MOON PHASE
8
Keitaro Arima
D1231234

Story So Far

Kouhei Mido has never had a close encounter with the supernatural kind, so why are ghosts showing up in every picture he takes? It all makes sense when he meets the adorable vampire girl Hazuki at an old German castle. After a treacherous battle against Count Kinkle, who was bent on capturing Hazuki for himself, Kouhei and his family thought they were finally safe.

While Kouhei and Hazuki seek refuge in the mountains to train and become stronger, Oyakata-sama sends a few new villains to stir up trouble-- a mysterious girl of incredible power, Art, and her hulking henchman, Balgus. Their target is Hazuki, but during a wild battle of magic, Hikaru gets kidnapped instead...!

TSUKUYOMI

Moon Phase

CREATED BY: KEITARO ARIMA

TOKYOPOP®

HAMBURG // LONDON // LOS ANGELES // TOKYO

Tsukuyomi: Moon Phase Volume 8

Created by Keitaro Arima

Translation - Yoohae Yang
English Adaptation - Jeffrey Reeves
Retouch and Lettering - Star Print Brokers
Production Artist - Bowen Park
Graphic Designer - Colin Graham

Editor - Katherine Schilling
Digital Imaging Manager - Chris Buford
Pre-Production Supervisor - Erika Terriquez
Art Director - Anne Marie Horne
Production Manager - Elisabeth Brizzi
Managing Editor - Vy Nguyen
VP of Production - Ron Klamert
Editor-in-Chief - Rob Tokar
Publisher - Mike Kiley
President and C.O.O. - John Parker
C.E.O. and Chief Creative Officer - Stuart Levy

A TOKYOPOP Manga

TOKYOPOP and [logo] are trademarks or registered trademarks of TOKYOPOP Inc.

TOKYOPOP Inc.
5900 Wilshire Blvd. Suite 2000
Los Angeles, CA 90036

E-mail: info@TOKYOPOP.com
Come visit us online at www.TOKYOPOP.com

© 2004 Keitaro Arima. All Rights Reserved. First published in 2004 by Wani Books., Tokyo, Japan.

English text copyright © 2007 TOKYOPOP Inc.

All rights reserved. No portion of this book may be reproduced or transmitted in any form or by any means without written permission from the copyright holders. This manga is a work of fiction. Any resemblance to actual events or locales or persons, living or dead, is entirely coincidental.

ISBN: 978-1-59532-955-4

First TOKYOPOP printing: September 2007

10 9 8 7 6 5 4 3 2 1

Printed in the USA

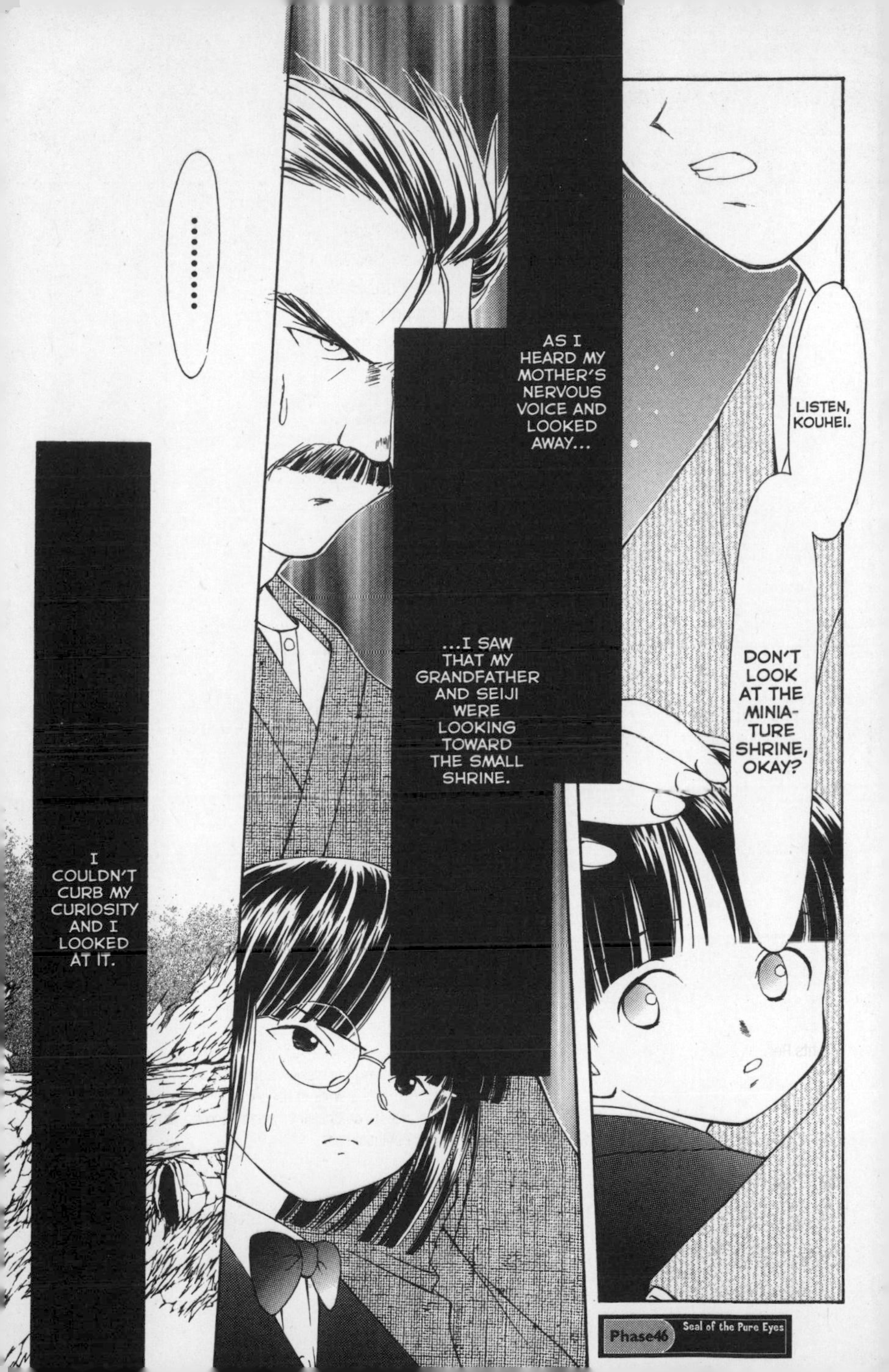
LISTEN, KOUHEI.
DON'T LOOK AT THE MINIA-TURE SHRINE, OKAY?
AS I HEARD MY MOTHER'S NERVOUS VOICE AND LOOKED AWAY...
...I SAW THAT MY GRANDFATHER AND SEIJI WERE LOOKING TOWARD THE SMALL SHRINE.
....
I COULDN'T CURB MY CURIOSITY AND I LOOKED AT IT.
Phase46 Seal of the Pure Eyes

THERE WAS JUST ONE SMALL SHRINE IN THE FIELD.
IN MY MEMORY, THAT DAY, I FELT ALIENATED FROM MY FAMILY.

Phase46 Seal of the Pure Eyes

ちら
......
THIS IS TERRIBLE!
I'M BEING KEPT IN THIS HOLE AS A HOSTAGE!
ズ~ン
S-SEIJI-SAMA...
WE MUST RUN!
NOW!
THE MOST SHOCKING THING WAS...

はっ
...THAT I WET MYSELF!!
Eh?!
ポロ
ポロ
...HE FOUND OUT...
....
ブン
ブン
Oh nooo!

A PURE GIRL WHO IS LOST IN HER THOUGHTS.
WHAT A BEAUTI-FUL THING.
?!
PLEASE.
YOU DON'T HAVE TO BE SCARED OF ME.
I WILL ELIMINATE...
...ALL OF YOUR WORRIES.

NOW, LOOK INTO MY EYES.
GASP!
TAKE A GOOD LOOK.
OH...

パタン
ALL RIGHT.
SHE WILL NOT WAKE UNTIL AN OUTSIDER TRIES TO REACH HER.
SORRY TO TROUBLE YOU, JEDA.
SHE WAS TOO NOISY.
IT WOULD HAVE BEEN EASIER TO SIMPLY TURN THE GIRL INTO ONE OF YOUR SERVANTS.
WHY DO YOU CARE TO KEEP A PROMISE WITH HUMANS?
NOW THAT I LOOK AT HER, SHE SEEMS MORE USEFUL.
I WOULD LOVE TO TAKE HER IN.
IDIOT!
?!

WHATEVER HAPPENS TO THIS GIRL, LUNA-SAMA WILL KNOW. DISTANCE DOES NOT MAKE A DIFFER-ENCE.
WHAT ARE WE GOING TO DO WITHOUT A HOSTAGE, IDIOT?!
......
YOU ARE RIGHT, SIR.
ペコリ
PLEASE, FORGIVE ME.

AL-THOUGH ...
...WE DON'T HAVE TO WAIT UNTIL THE PROMISED DAY.
WE MUST TAKE SUITABLE ACTION SOON.
......

BAL-
GUS
...?
WILL MY FATHER GET MAD AT ME...
...IF I KILL LUNA?
ユラ
ユラ
YES, INDEED. THAT WILL MAKE HIM VERY UPSET, PRIN-
CESS.
......

I WILL KILL HIM...
...IN FRONT OF LUNA.
AS YOU WISH.
THEN, I'LL FOR-GET ABOUT LUNA FOR NOW.
BUT I WANT THAT MAN.
....

WHAT...?
I'M A "KENKI"? AS IN...A MAN WITH PURE EYES?!

THAT'S RIGHT.
WHEN YOU WERE BORN, WE FOUND OUT THAT YOU ARE A KENKI. GIFTED WITH THE ABILITY TO SEE GHOSTS AND DEMONS.
....
WHAT'S A "KENKI"?
JUST WHAT WE SAID. "ONE WHO SEES DEMONS."
?!
HE IS A MEDIUM.
WHAT ?!
ARE YOU SERI-OUS ?!
IT'S TRUE.

TO HIM, THINGS OF THIS WORLD AND THE NEXT ARE ONE AND THE SAME.
EVEN AS A BABE, HE WAS CLEARLY UNIQUE.
THEREFORE, RYUHEI, HIS MOTHER SHIZURU, AND I WERE VERY CONCERNED ABOUT HIM.
RYU-HEI? WHO'S THAT?
ボッ ボッ
HE'S TALKING ABOUT MY GRAND-FATHER.
HAZUKI.
HAVE YOU EVER THOUGHT THAT KOUHEI'S SENSITIVITY WAS DULL?
?!
ピト
ALL THE TIME!
?!
HE'S GOT THE DULLEST SENSITIVITY IN THE WORLD!

TUUUUG
OWW! OUCH !!
IN FACT, HE DOESN'T NOTICE ANYTHING AT ALL!
DARN YOU, KOUHEI!
I SEE.
HOWEVER, THAT IS TO BE EXPECTED IN HIS CASE.
THAT ALSO EXPLAINS HIS ABILITY TO READ "KI" USING HIS SIXTH SENSE.
WE SEALED ...
...KOUHEI'S PSYCHIC SENSE, SO HE CAN'T USE IT.

WHAT?!
WHY?!
BASICALLY, WE SHUT DOWN THE STREAM OF "KI," THE SPIRITUAL ENERGY THAT RELATES TO THE PSYCHIC SENSE.
AND WE USED "KOTODAMA", THE SOUL OF LANGUAGE, SO HE WOULDN'T DIRECT HIS ATTENTION TO GHOSTS.
KOUHEI, DO YOU REMEMBER BEING TOLD OVER AND OVER SINCE CHILDHOOD HOW YOUR FATHER WAS A NORMAL PHOTOGRAPHER, AND HOW YOU LACKED THE PSYCHIC ABILITY THE REST OF US HAVE?
WE WERE TRYING TO DIVERT YOUR ATTENTION AWAY FROM GHOSTS AND SPIRITS.
WHY?
YOU DON'T UNDER-STAND YET?
WHAT WOULD OTHER PEOPLE THINK IF THEY SAW A CHILD TALKING TO THIN AIR?

AN ALIEN EXIST-ENCE WILL ONLY RESULT IN...
...FEAR AND EX-CLUSION OR REJECT-ION.
ESPECIALLY BECAUSE YOUR PSYCHIC SENSE IS STRONGLY INTERACTIVE.
THAT MEANS THAT GHOSTS AND SPIRITS COULD SEE YOU AS YOU COULD SEE THEM.
NO MATTER HOW MUCH OTHERS AROUND YOU TRY TO PROTECT YOU...
...THERE IS A GREATER POSSIBILITY OF A DEMONIC POSSESS-ION.
SHIZURU, YOUR MOTHER, WAS ESPECIALLY WORRIED ABOUT IT. EVEN AFTER YOU LOST YOUR PSYCHIC ABILITY, SHE COULDN'T STOP WORRYING ABOUT YOU.
......

I REMEMBER HOW...
...SOMETIMES MY MOTHER SEEMED TO BE SCARED OF AN EMPTY SPACE AND TOLD ME NOT TO GO NEAR IT.
I COULDN'T UNDERSTAND WHY SHE WAS LIKE THAT.
......
WAR
IT MADE ME SAD BECAUSE I DIDN'T UNDERSTAND WHY.
KOUHEI!
COME BACK HERE!
KOUHEI!

THAT'S WHY I...
THERE'S NOTHING!
THERE IS NOTHING HERE TO FEAR!

HEY, KOU-KUN?
...JUST WANTED TO BELIEVE...
?
WHAT IS IT, SEI-CHAN?
IT'S NOT THAT THERE'S NOTHING THERE...
IT'S THAT YOU MAY HAVE ERASED THEM.
...THAT THERE WAS NOTHING.

UNTIL I SUCCEED IN COMPLETELY UNSEALING KOUHEI'S ABILITY...
...YOU MUST NOT SEE KOUHEI!
YOU HEAR ME?
BUT...
WHY IS THIS HAPPENING TO ME?!
WHYYY?!
I DON'T UNDERSTAND WHY!!

HOW COME ONLY KAORU WAS ASKED TO HELP YAYOI-SAMA?!
WHAT IN THE WORLD IS GOING ON HERE?!
......
YOUR "ELIMINATING POWER" WILL BE USELESS...
...IN YOUR FIGHT AGAINST THE VAMPIRES.

FIRST, YOU MUST LEARN HOW TO DISTIN- GUISH WHICH POWER TO ELIMINATE.
PREPARE YOURSELF, FOR I WILL NOW UNSEAL YOUR PURE EYES.

Moon 月詠 Phase

"SPIRITUAL CHANGE" IS DIFFICULT AND IN ORDER TO FOCUS IT, YOU MUST TAKE THE PROPER RITUALS.
AUSTERE DISCIPLINE OF PRAYER
THE RITUAL IS TO ASSURE THAT THE PERSON HAS PRO-GRESSED ENOUGH...
FIRE WALKING
...TO CONTROL THE SPIRITUAL ENERGY BETWEEN HIMSELF AND THE SUPER-NATURAL.
KOUHEI, ARE YOU READY?
Phase47 The Price of Erasing Power

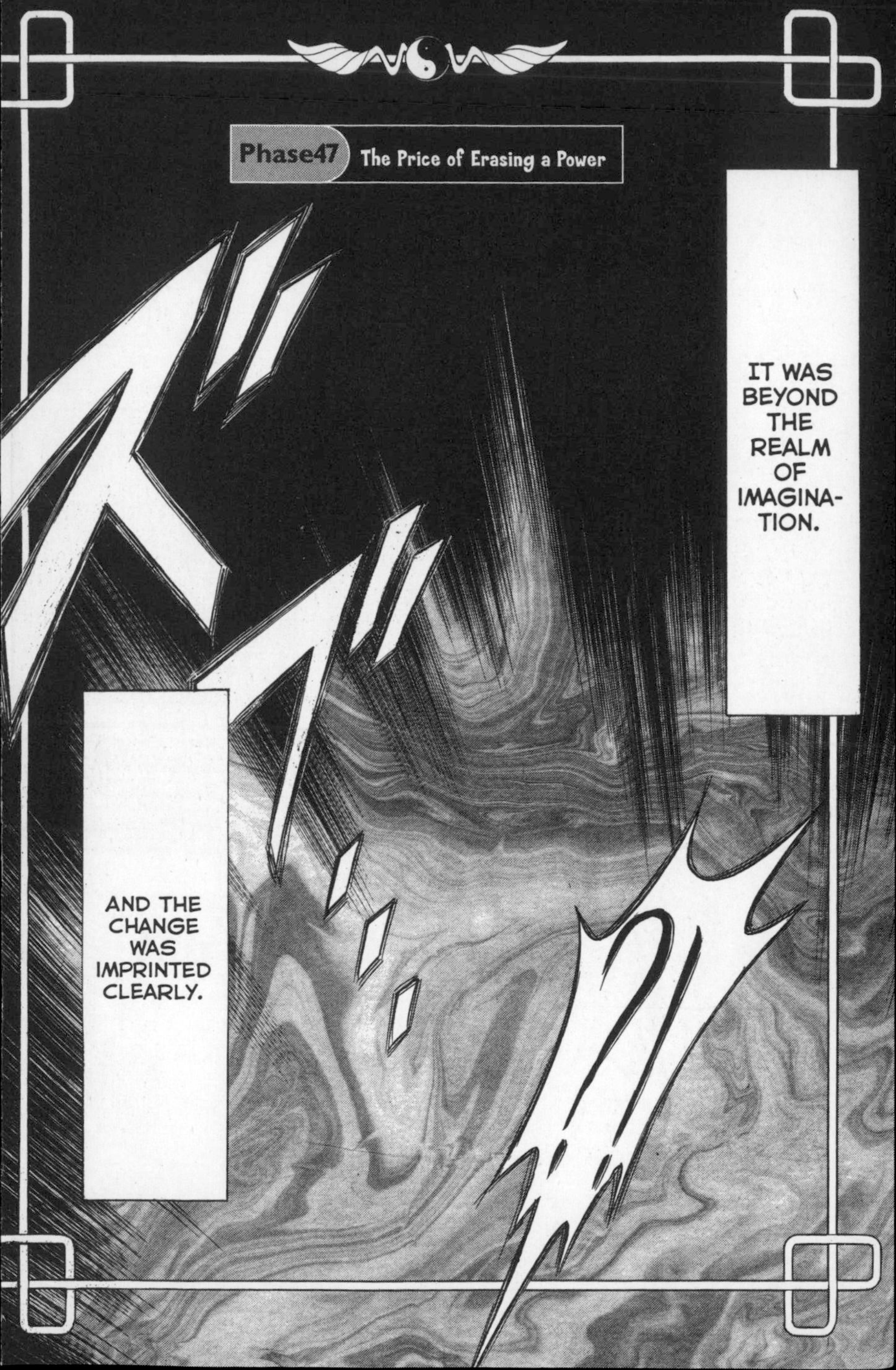
Phase47 The Price of Erasing a Power
IT WAS BEYOND THE REALM OF IMAGINA-TION.
AND THE CHANGE WAS IMPRINTED CLEARLY.

UH...
?!
OH...
...!
HAZUKI?
OH, MY.
HOW RUDE, KOUHEI-NIISAMA.
AFTER ALL THE TIME...
...I'VE SPENT TAKING CARE OF YOU.

K-KAORU?
YES?
THAT'S ME.
I WILL GO GET YAYOI-SAMA.
Am I dreaming? She actually talks!
?
scrtch
scrtch
scrtch
scrtch
WHAT'S THAT SOUND?
GRINDING ITS TEETH
scrtch
scrtch

W-WAIT A MIN-UTE.
WHY DO I HAVE THE FEELING I'VE SEEN THIS BEFORE?
Aaaah!
Aaaah!
Waaah!
Ooh!
ギョロ
......
EW!
HUH?!

GYAA!
WH- WHAT WAS THAT?!
Gya!
Gya! Gya!
THAT WAS A PARTIAL POWER OF YOU "ERASING" ABILITY.
MAS- TER?
YUP!
SO, HOW ARE YOU FEEL- ING?

HOW DO YOU THINK I FEEL?
MY EYES FEEL LIKE THEY WERE JUST PULLED OUT AND PINCHED!
Gya!
Ha ha ha.
BUT I'M SURE YOU CAN SEE BETTER NOW, RIGHT?
YOU ARE SEEING A FORMLESS MONSTER RIGHT NOW.
So cruel!
EH?
AFTER YOUR HARD TRAINING, YOU'RE NOW CAPABLE OF SEEING THEM VAGUELY.
THIS IS THE MONSTER I USED DURING THE LAST TRAINING TEST.

Aaaaaah!
IT WAS MUCH BIGGER LAST TIME.
OH...
HE MUST BE TALKING ABOUT THE FOG-LIKE THING I SAW.
UNTIL NOW, YOU HAVE ELIMINATED ALL KINDS OF "SPIRITUAL SUBSTANCE" UNCONSCIOUSLY.
FROM NOW ON, YOU'LL NEED TO CHOOSE A TARGET CONSCIOUSLY IN ORDER TO ELIMINATE IT.
THIS MONSTER IS CALLED "STARVING ANIMA."
IT ABSORBS ACTIVE ENERGY AROUND ITSELF AND IT IS CAPABLE OF DUPLICATING AND INCREASING ITS MASS.
SO IT IS VERY USEFUL IN THAT KIND OF TEST.
FIRST, I WANT YOU TO...
...TRY TO ERASE THIS MONSTER.

E-
ERASE
IT?!
HOW CAN I ERASE A CREATURE THAT HAS A "CLEAR EXISTENCE" ?!
Aaah...
Aaah...
BY WILL-POWER!
ALTHOUGH WE CAN SEE THEM, THEY ARE ERASABLE.
YOU MUST CREATE THE RIGHT CONSCIOUS-NESS FOR THAT FIRST.
AND YOU MUST ACT ON IT AS QUICKLY AS YOU CAN.
KOUHEI-NIISAMA?
YES, KAORU?

I AM VERY GLAD TO BE ABLE TO COMMUNICATE WITH YOU BY USING TELEPATHY.
I LIKE YOU VERY MUCH AND YOU ARE A VERY IMPORTANT PERSON TO ME.
They are your future husbands.
squeal!
AFTER ALL...
...I'VE ALWAYS DREAMED OF GETTING MARRIED TO YOU SOME-DAY.
BUT...
...IF I CAN'T DO ANYTHING...
...AND I CAN'T EVEN HELP HIKARU...

...I SOME-TIMES WONDER ...
...IF IT IS BETTER FOR ME TO BE EATEN BY THESE MON-STERS.

SIGH...
WAAAHHHH!
KOUHEI...
WHAT ARE YOU DOING NOW?

WELL...
THAT'S ENOUGH FOR TODAY.
HUFF
HUFF
BYE, KOUHEI-NIISAMA! ♡
SEE YOU TOMOR-ROW!
HUFF
HUFF

グッテ〜
I CAN'T BELIEVE IT!
WHEN I SAID SO EASILY...
..."THEY DON'T EXIST!!"...
...I NEVER EXPECTED I'D BE ABLE TO ERASE THEM SO EASILY, TOO!
IT'S SO DIFFI-CULT TO CON-TROL.
KAORU!
ARE YOU ALL RIGHT?!
Y-YES.
I AM SORRY.

DON'T PUSH YOUR LIMIT.
THOSE MONSTERS ARE NORMALLY HARD TO CONTROL.
I'M ALL RIGHT.
I GET ALONG WITH THEM.
KOUHEI-NIISAMA IS DOING HIS BEST.
MOST IMPORTANT-LY, THIS IS FOR HIKARU.
BUT ...
... I'M A LITTLE ...
...TIRED.
Zzz...
......

THREE DAYS LATER...
TELL ME ONE GOOD REASON...
...WHY I CAN'T SEE KOUHEI!!
がう
HAZUKI, LISTEN TO ME.
HE IS IN THE MIDDLE OF DIFFICULT TRAINING.
AS HIS WISH TO SEE YOU GROWS...
...THAT DESIRE WILL BECOME HIS POWER TO MOTIVATE HIMSELF DURING TRAINING.
I UNDER-STAND YOU ARE WORRIED ABOUT HIM.
BUT YOU MUST BE PATIENT RIGHT NOW.
....

……
トボ
トボ
OH, KOUHEI ...
ARE YOU BEHIND THIS WALL?
ス

HAZUKI?
ARE YOU THERE?
EH?!
WHAT?!
KOUHEI!
H-HOW DID YOU KNOW IT WAS ME?!
MY SENSE IS BECOMING SHARPER LATELY.
I KNEW IT WAS YOU RIGHT AWAY. I FELT A DIFFERENT SORT OF PRESENCE FROM THE OTHER THREE.
HA HA HA...
HOW HAVE YOU BEEN?
......

OKAY, I GUESS.
I WAS JUST THINKING HOW I SHOULD PUMMEL YOU NEXT TIME I SEE YOU!
I'VE FINALLY STARTED TO GRASP THE TECHNIQUE OF ERASING.
THOUGH I MUST HURRY TO LEARN IT. I'M CAUSING TROUBLES TO MASTER AND KAORU.
......
KOU-HEI.
I...
WHILE EVERY-ONE IS DOING HIS OR HER BEST TO RESCUE HIKARU...
...I'VE BEEN SO USE-LESS.
I'M SORRY.
I SEE.
Ha ha ha!

I'M SO SORRY.
YOU...
...HAVE BEEN USEFUL.
YOU'RE THE REASON I'M WORKING SO HARD.
RIGHT?!
MASTER?!
THANK YOU.
I WANT TO SEE YOU, KOUHEI.
NO! WE CAN'T!

NO ...?!
WHAT DO YOU MEAN BY THAT?!
DIDN'T MASTER TELL YOU NOT TO SEE ME DURING TRAINING?
I...
I KNOW, BUT...
LET'S PUT OUR FEEL-INGS ON HOLD FOR NOW!
!....
OKAY.
?!
BY THE WAY...
...I'M GOING TO WALK THROUGH THE CONNECTING CORRIDOR TO THE BATHROOM.
ポリ
ポリ
ON THE WAY TO THE BATH-ROOM ...
...WHO KNOWS, I MAY PASS SOME-ONE.

O-OF COURSE!
IT HAPPENS ALL THE TIME, RIGHT?
ドタ
ドタ
ドタ
......
ポリ
Do I spoil her too much?
OF COURSE, I SHOULD HAVE THOUGHT THIS THROUGH.
ガラララッ
I REALLY DIDN'T THINK ABOUT WHY MASTER DIDN'T WANT US TO SEE EACH OTHER.
I THOUGHT THAT JUST SEEING EACH OTHER COULDN'T HURT THE PROGRESS OF TRAINING.
KOU-HEI!

WHEN SUDDEN-LY...
KOU-HEI! ♡
..."IT" CAME INTO MY SIGHT.

THE EVIL, ENORMOUS "IT" WAS THE IMAGE OF...
...HAZUKI'S KARMA.
WAAAAAAA!
AH!!

Moon 月詠 Phase

NOOOO! GO AWAY!!
KOU-HEI!
WHAT'S WRONG?! KOUHEI?!
Phase48 The important "Timing"

Phase48 The important "Timing"
KOU-HEI!
WAAAHHH!!

I HAD TO PUT HIM INTO SLEEP.
I HOPE HE'LL BE CALM WHEN HE WAKES UP.
Y-YAYOI-SAMA!
WHAT'S WRONG WITH KOUHEI?!
I'VE NEVER SEEN KOUHEI LIKE THAT!

KOUHEI WAS...
...SUCKED INTO HIS FEAR.
NORMALLY PEOPLE CAN'T SEE...
...THE ENTITY OF AN ASTRAL BODY AND LIFE ENERGY.
WE EXPECTED THIS NEGATIVE CONSE-QUENCE...
...WHEN WE SEALED KOUHEI'S PSYCHIC ABILITY.
SINCE WE FEEL THOSE EXISTEN-CES...
...WE "VISUALIZE" THE IMAGE BASED ON OUR EXPERIENCE AND KNOWLEDGE FROM THE PAST.

ON SUCH OCCASIONS ...
...WE NEED AN ABILITY TO FIGURE OUT WHAT EXACTLY THE INVISIBLE "ENTITY" IS.
?
BY THE WAY, HAZUKI...
YES?
I AM VERY ANGRY WITH YOU AND KOUHEI FOR SEEING EACH OTHER.
DO YOU UNDERSTAND WHAT IT MEANS?
EH?!
YES! UM...
OH!
......
I'M REALLY VERY SORRY!
I'M JUST KIDDING.

?!
うるうる
JUST NOW... ALTHOUGH I DIDN'T CHANGE MY FACIAL EXPRESSION...
...THE IMPRESSION YOU GET FROM ME WAS CHANGED BY MY WORDS ASSOCIATED WITH A DIFFERENT SITUATION, RIGHT?
JUST LIKE WORDS, INFORMATION FROM DOING "REISHI," OR SEEING AND FEELING GHOSTS, DOESN'T HAVE SUBSTANCE. THEREFORE WHOEVER RECEIVES IT CAN CHANGE THE FORM INSIDE OF THEIR MINDS.
BUT EVEN IF THE EXISTENCE CAN ONLY BE RECOGNIZED BY THE ABILITY OF REISHI, WITH TRAININGS AND EXPERIENCES, IT IS POSSIBLE TO ALTER THE CHANGE WITHOUT DESTROYING THE ACTUAL FIGURE.
BUT IT HAS ONLY BEEN THREE DAYS SINCE KOUHEI LEARNED HOW TO DO REISHI.
THEREFORE, KOUHEI COULDN'T YET CONTROL THE IMAGE THAT'S ASSOCIATED WITH YOU.
?!

MY IMAGE?
DO YOU MEAN THAT KOUHEI IS SCARED OF ME?
HE'S COMING!
WITH DEATH ...!
HE IS COMING...!
UGH...

UH ...
IT IS... BRINGING-ING...
HUFF ...
LOOK. IT'S WAITING FOR YOU...
HUFF ...
HUFF ...
IT'S NOT...
HUFF ...
...LIKE THAT.
I...
HUFF ...
I LO... HER...

?!!
DON'T YOU RE-MEMBER ...
...WHAT HAPPENED TO YOU AND YOUR FAMILY?
AH!
AAAH!
GRAND-PA!

YOUR GRAND-FATHER IS DEAD NOW.
AND YOU...
YOU ARE NEXT!
KOUHEI!
AH!
WAH!

WAAAH!!
WAIT! KOU-HEI!
YOU'RE NOT SCARED OF ME, ARE YOU?
YOU LOVE ME...
...AND YOU WILL PROTECT ME!
TELL ME!
ガチ ガチ
ブルルッ
ガタ ガタ

N-NO!
DON'T ...!
DON'T COME NEAR ME!
KOUHEI ...
PRESSING HIM FOR ANSWERS LIKE THIS...
...WON'T SOLVE HIS SITUA-TION.
YAYOI-SAMA!
DON'T COME CLOSER ...

IN THESE TWO YEARS...
...KOUHEI HAS PUT A LOT OF EFFORT INTO BECOMING STRONGER.
HE WAS DESPE-RATE TO BECOME STRONG-ER...
...TO PROTECT YOU AND AVENGE HIS GRAND-FATHER'S DEATH.
BUT RIGHT NOW...
...HIS WISH BACKFIRED ON HIM.
......
HIS DESPERA-TION SHOWS...
...THAT HE HAS A REASON TO BE DRIVEN TO BE STONGER.
IT IS PROOF THAT HE HAS "FEAR" AND "WORRY."

AS MUCH AS YOU ARE AN IMPORTANT PERSON WHO KOUHEI WANTS TO PROTECT WITH HIS LIFE...
YAYOI-SAMA?
YES?
...YOU ARE ALSO THE SYMBOL OF SOMETHING FEARFUL THAT HAS ENDANGERED KOUHEI'S LIFE.
IF KOUHEI DIDN'T MEET ME...
...HE WOULDN'T HAVE TO GO THROUGH THIS, WOULD HE?

FROM THE BEGINNING, IT WAS A HIGH-STAKES GAMBLE.
NOT EXACTLY.

I WILL LEAVE YOUR MEAL RIGHT HERE.
YOU'VE LOST A LOT OF WEIGHT.

I KEEP SEEING THE FIGURE OF HAZUKI IN MY HEAD AND I CAN'T STOP TREMBLING.
KOHARU-SAN...
I'M TERRI-FIED.
OH, REALLY.
I SEE. HAZUKI-CHAN IS A VERY PRECIOUS PERSON TO YOU.
BUT MY GRANDDAUGHTERS WON'T BE TOO HAPPY TO HEAR THAT.
Ho ho ho...
I DON'T KNOW WHY...
...BUT I'M SO SCARED OF HER.
WHEN I SAW HER FOR THE FIRST TIME...

WHEN SHE SUCKED MY BLOOD ...
I KEEP RE-MEMBER-ING...
...ALL KINDS OF THINGS.
...
THOSE MEMORIES ARE SPINNING IN MY HEAD.

EVER SINCE I MET HAZUKI...
...I'M ALWAYS THINKING ABOUT HER.
SHE'S ANNOYING, BUT SHE'S SO CUTE.
I JUST WANTED TO BE WITH HER.
I GOT SO DESPERATE...
BUT...
...I UNDERSTAND SOMETHING NOW.

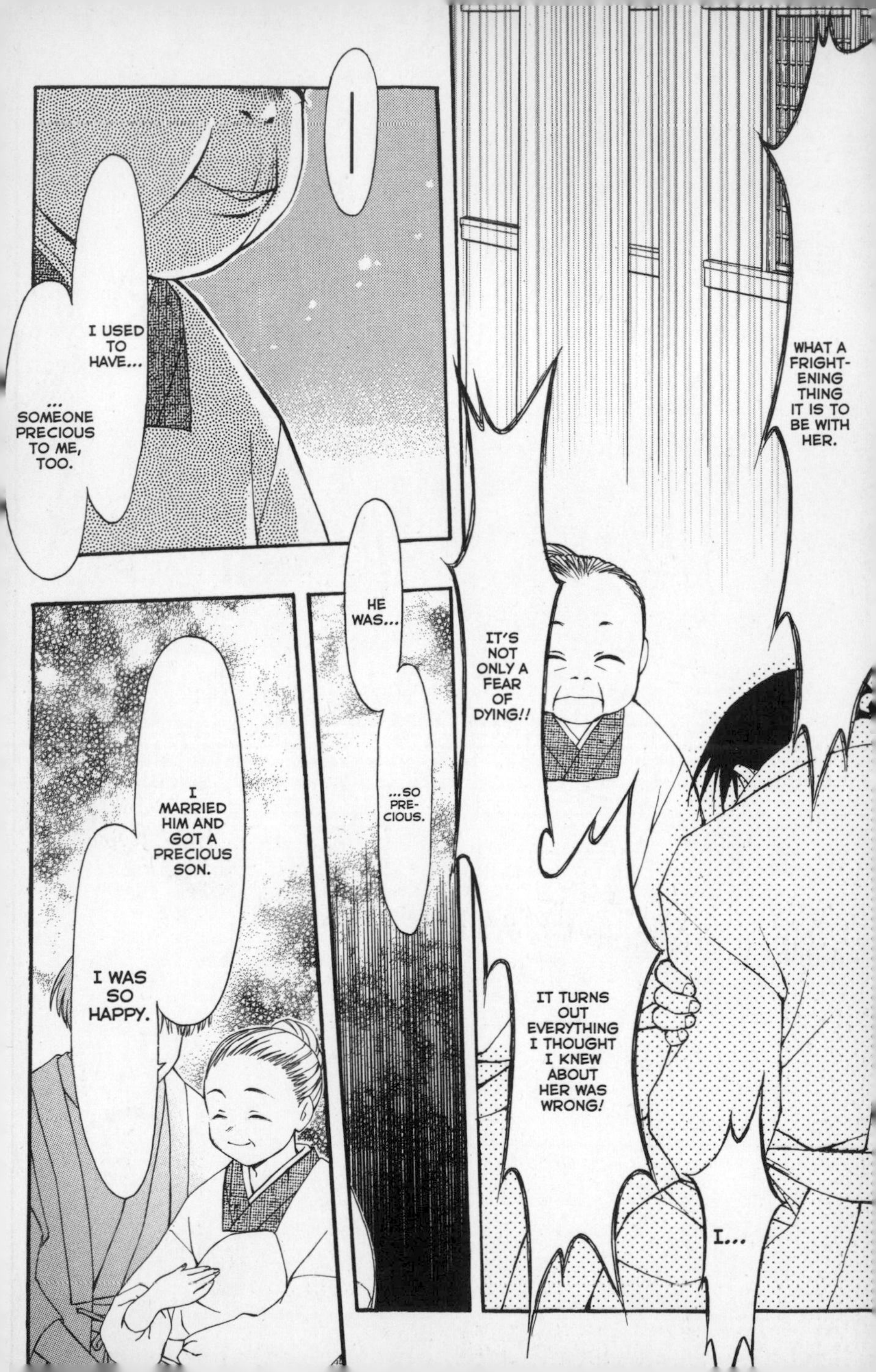
WHAT A FRIGHT-ENING THING IT IS TO BE WITH HER.
IT'S NOT ONLY A FEAR OF DYING!!
IT TURNS OUT EVERYTHING I THOUGHT I KNEW ABOUT HER WAS WRONG!
I...
—
I USED TO HAVE...
...SOMEONE PRECIOUS TO ME, TOO.
HE WAS...
...SO PRE-CIOUS.
I MARRIED HIM AND GOT A PRECIOUS SON.
I WAS SO HAPPY.

FOR SOME REASON, HE SEEMED SO LIGHT, LIKE HE WAS FLOATING.
I USED TO THINK THAT HE WOULD FLY AWAY SOMEDAY.
BUT HE ALWAYS TOOK CARE OF THINGS FOR ME WHEN I NEEDED HIM.
YOU SHARE THE SAME BLOOD-LINE AS HIM.
I BELIEVE IN YOU...
...AND TRUST THAT YOU WILL NOT MISS THE IMPOR-TANCE OF "TIMING."

I SEE.
I DIDN'T KNOW KOUHEI WENT THROUGH SUCH A THING.
SO HE CAN'T BE RELIED ON AS A GOOD WARRIOR.
HOW ABOUT YOU, SEIJI?
UN-FORTU-NATELY...
...WE CAN'T EXPECT ANY REINFORCE-MENTS.

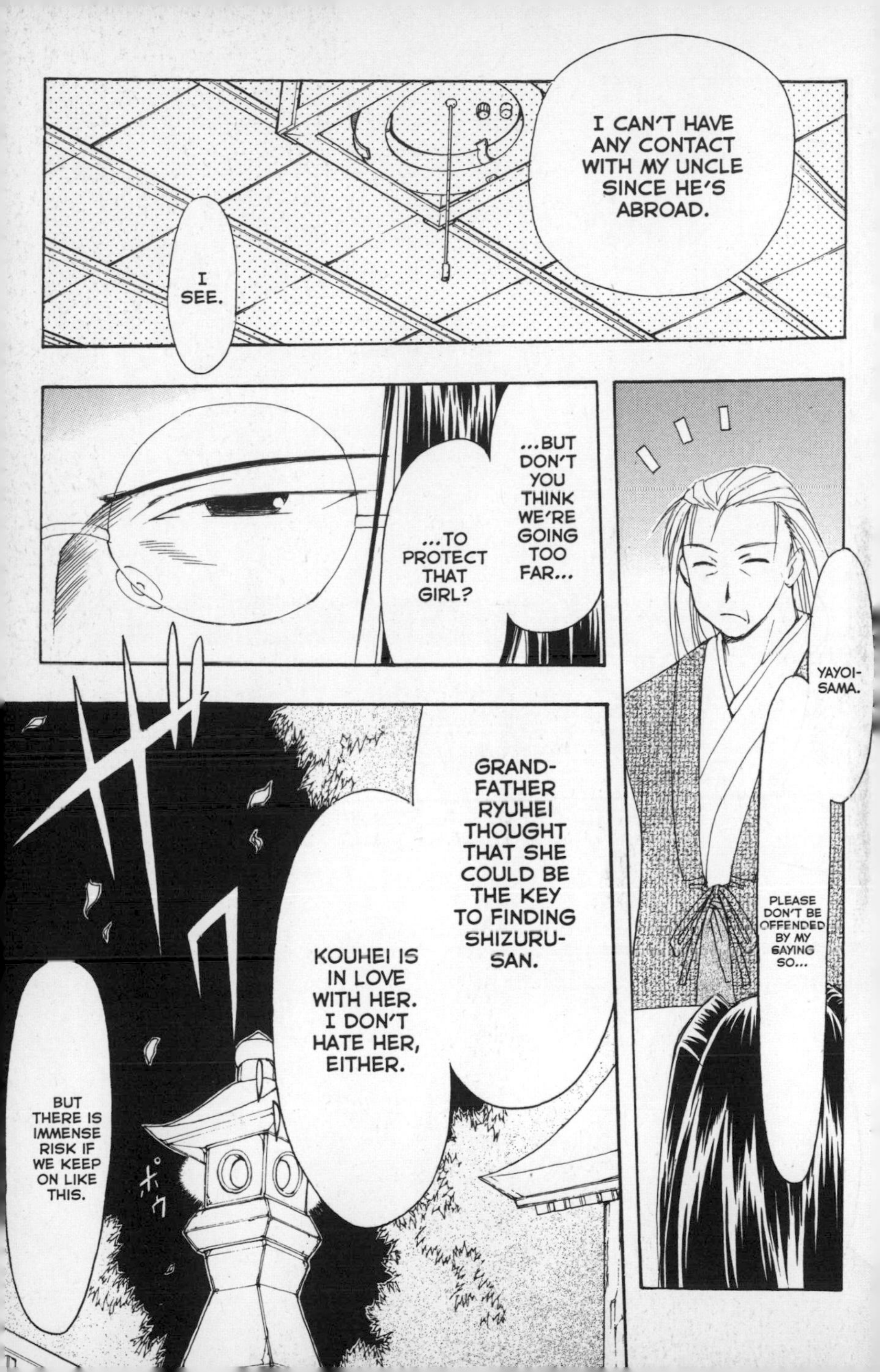
I CAN'T HAVE ANY CONTACT WITH MY UNCLE SINCE HE'S ABROAD.
I SEE.
YAYOI-SAMA.
PLEASE DON'T BE OFFENDED BY MY SAYING SO...
...BUT DON'T YOU THINK WE'RE GOING TOO FAR...
...TO PROTECT THAT GIRL?
GRAND-FATHER RYUHEI THOUGHT THAT SHE COULD BE THE KEY TO FINDING SHIZURU-SAN.
KOUHEI IS IN LOVE WITH HER. I DON'T HATE HER, EITHER.
BUT THERE IS IMMENSE RISK IF WE KEEP ON LIKE THIS.
ポク

ニヤッ
?!
BE CARE-FUL!
SOMEONE BROKE INTO MY KEKKAI!
?!
バッ
NO... I CAN'T ...
I...
I DON'T...

I DON'T WANT TO GO DOWN TOGETHER!
WHAT IS THIS?!
OH... DON'T BE AFRAID.
THIS IS A PLACE WHERE YOU CAN HEAR THE VOICE OF YOUR MIND.

AMONG ALL OF YOUR DOUBTS...
...I WILL HELP YOU TO CHOOSE ONE TRUTH.

Phase49 Invasion! Jeda's Magic Eyes
......
I SENSE SOME-THING!
IT'S DIFFERENT FROM THE OTHERS!
?!
A CAT GIRL WHO IS WORRIED ABOUT KOUHEI AND WAITING RIGHT BY THE SHRINE.

ポウー
ポウッ
WHAT?!
AUGH!

Phase49 Invasion! Jeda's Magic Eyes
AAAARGH!

DID THE DEMON-SEALING DOLLS...
...WORK ON HIM?
I HOPE SO.
YAYOI-SAMA!
WHAT WAS THAT?!
......

IT IS ONE OF YOUR PEOPLE.
WHAT?
DIDN'T YOU HEAR ME?
A "VAMPIRE" JUST LIKE YOU...
...CAME TO GET YOU.
SEIJI-SAN ...?
YOU MUST HAVE ALREADY FIGURED IT OUT, HAVEN'T YOU?

YOU ARE TOO DIFFERENT FROM US.
IT'S IMPOSSIBLE FOR US TO BE TOGETHER!

WHY DON'T YOU JUST...
SEIJI ...
YOU ARE POS-SESS-ED BY THE DEVIL.
WHAT?! ME?!
WHAT I'M SAYING IS LOGICAL!
...LEAVE WITH YOUR PEOPLE?
IT'S BEST FOR HER TO JUST LEAVE WITH HER PEOPLE!
....
NO...
YOU CAN'T.

HIKARU WON'T BE ABLE TO COME HOME ...
...IF YOU LET HER GO.
UGH!
YOUR LIFE IS...
...IN DANGER.
WHAT ARE YOU THINKING?!
JUST REST FOR A WHILE.
SEIJI.

AAH!
HA HA...
HA HA HA...
I GUESS IT WON'T BE TOO EASY, HUH?
....
IF IT WAS POS-SIBLE...
...I WANTED TO GO EASY ON YOU.
BUT YOU'VE GIVEN ME NO CHOICE NOW.

MY NAME IS JE-DA.
I HOPE YOU RE-MEMBER ME.
I AM "KUGUTSU-SHI" JEDA, ONE WHO CAN CONTROL MINDS.
HAZUKI! GO GET KOUHEI'S BLOOD!!
YES, MASTER!

EVIL EYES!
WHAT?!
WELL ...
IT DIDN'T REACH LADY LUNA.
I GUESS I'LL JUST HAVE TO DO MY BEST HERE.
HOW CAN HE...?
I THOUGHT I SET THE PROTECTION AGAINST EVIL EYES!
ARE YOU GUYS SUR-PRISED?
MY EVIL EYES ARE VERY SPECIAL.
Ergh!
Agh!
NO ONE HAS EVER ESCAPED MY EVIL EYES.

Ha ha ha...
It's quite impressive that you can even muster a groan after seeing my eyes.
Why...
...even the young lady hasn't said a thing.
ごぽ
Come out from there.
Eat as much as you want... starving animas...
WHAT?!

WHAT IS THIS ?!
WAAAAH!
MY FRIENDS ARE SAYING...
...THAT YOU TASTE PRETTY GOOD.
I SEE! YOU...!
......
YOUR EYES...!
YOU CAN'T SEE WITH YOUR EYES!

IT IS COMING!
IT'S COMING!
KOUHEI! IT'S AN EMERGENCY!
KOUHEI!
IT'S COMING! IT'S COMING!
THERE'S A NEW VAMPIRE!
KOUHEI!
IT IS COMING!
YAYOI-SAMA IS DOING HIS BEST TO KEEP HIM OUT THERE, BUT WE MUST DO SOME-THING!

KOUHEI!
PLEASE LET ME KISS YOU!
IT MEANS YOUR DEATH!
PLEASE!
WAAAAAH!

WAAAAAAAH!!
WAAHH!!
AAAAAH!
WAAAAH!!
AAAAH!!
LIAR!

KOUHEI, YOU LIAR!
PLEASE FIGHT WITH ME!
AH!
HIC
HIC
HELP...
?!
KOU-HEI?
HELP.
ブル
ブル
PLEASE ...
HELP ME...
SOME-BODY...

HELP...!
KOUHEI...
HA
...
HA
HA
HA
HA!

WERE YOU TRYING TO SUCK MY SPIRITUAL ENERGY?!
AMUSING!♡
ズイ..
HA HA HA HA ...

SINCE YOU'RE THE ONE WHO'S CONTROLLING THESE MONSTERS...
...BEFORE THEY SUCK ALL MY SPIRITUAL ENERGY...
...I WILL MAKE YOU MY SLAVE.
WAIT THERE ...
...FOR ME.
I'LL BE RIGHT THERE.
HA HA HA HA...

KAORU ...
ガク
ガク
ATTACK ME AND RUN!
HURRY ...
HOLD IT RIGHT THERE!

LADY LUNA...
YOU THERE!
DON'T HURT ANYONE HERE!
KAORU. PLEASE MAKE THOSE MONSTERS DISAPPEAR.
?!

I...
I'M GOING BACK TO MY PEOPLE.

Moon 月詠 Phase

I...
I'M GOING BACK TO MY PEOPLE.
I SEE.
FINALLY, LADY LUNA DECIDED TO COME HOME WITH US.
YES.
SHE SAID SHE WOULD COME HOME WITH US BY EXCHANGING THE GIRL ON THE APPOINTED DAY.
THERE IS ONE CONDITION.
Phase50 Good-bye, Kouhei...

WE MUST ASSURE THE SECURITY OF THE PEOPLE LADY LUNA MET.
Phase50
Good-bye, Kouhei...
Goodness.
IT'S AS IF WE WERE THE BAD GUYS, ISN'T IT?
......

PRINCESS. PLEASE WAIT.
WE WERE ORDERED TO BRING LADY LUNA TO OYAKATA-SAMA.
I UNDERSTAND THAT YOU DON'T LIKE THE SOUND OF THAT.
......
BUT YOU MUST FORGET ABOUT THE MAN...
...UNTIL WE COMPLETE OUR MISSION.

PRINCESS!
OH NO...
SHE'S SULKING NOW.
......

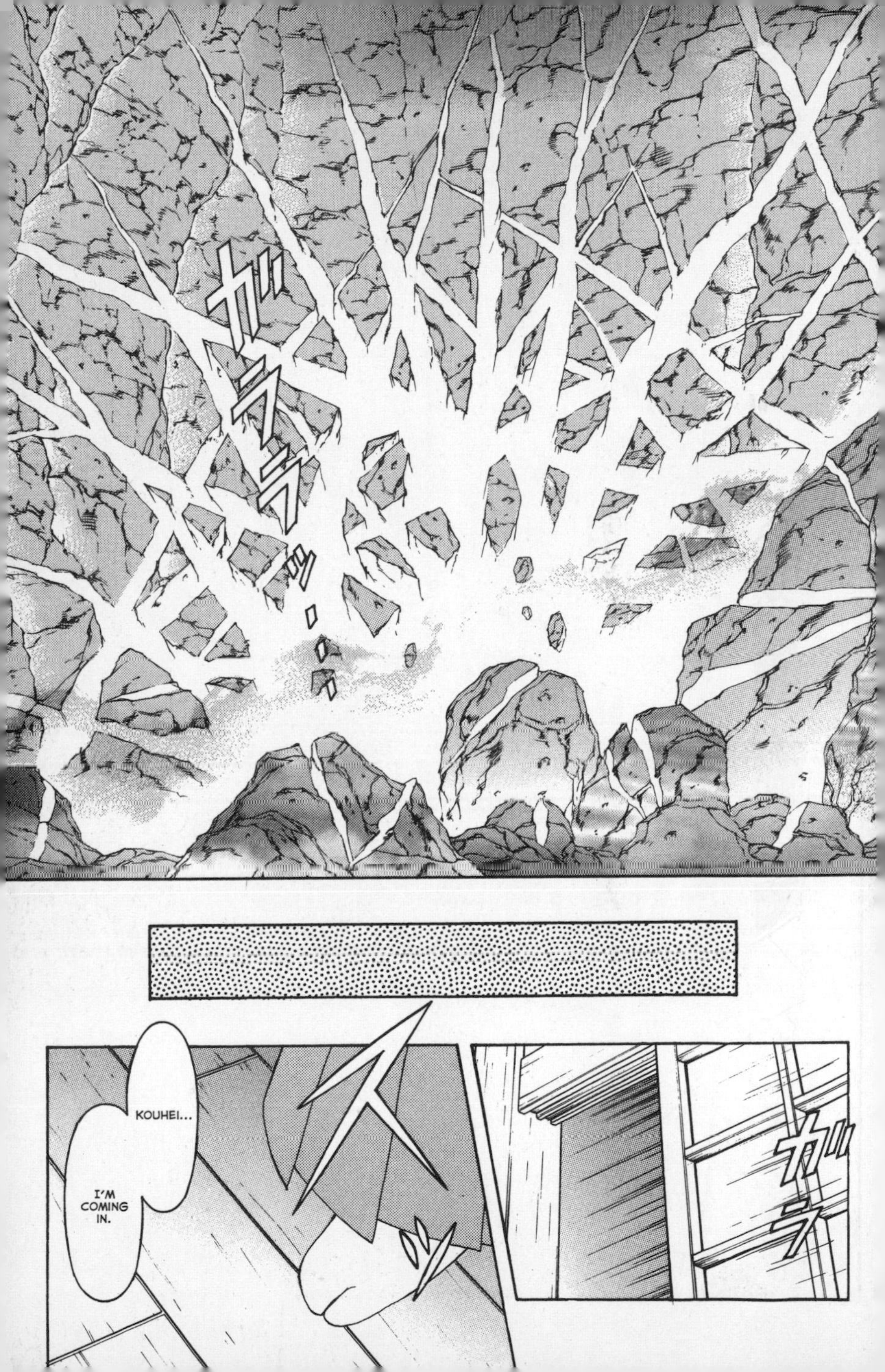
カラララ
KOUHEI...
I'M COMING IN.
ス
カラ

....
KOUHEI...

HUFF HUFF
HUFF
KOU-HEI...
I...I'M SORRY.
DON'T WORRY. YOU DON'T HAVE TO BE SCARED.
I WON'T COME ANY CLOSER.
I WON'T BE ABLE TO SEE YOU ANYMORE.
WHATEVER MAKES YOU SCARED WON'T BE HERE ANYMORE.
YOU'LL BE FINE.

HEY, DO YOU REMEMBER...
...THE FIRST TIME WE MET EACH OTHER?
AND I SUCKED YOUR BLOOD, BUT YOU NEVER LISTENED TO MY ORDERS.
I JUST WANTED TO GET OUT FROM THE CASTLE TO SEE MY MOTHER.
I WAS REALLY MAD AT YOU.

ALTHOUGH YOU WOULDN'T BECOME MY SLAVE, YOU STILL STAYED CLOSE TO ME.
SURE, YOU ALWAYS COMPLAIN...
...AND WE FIGHT A LOT...
...AND EVEN RIGHT NOW, YOU DON'T DO AS I TELL YOU.

...BEFORE I KNEW IT...I STOPPED MISSING MY MOTHER.
BUT...
...ALTHOUGH MY MOTHER MAY SCOLD ME FOR SAYING THIS...

BECAUSE YOUR GRAND-FATHER, ELFRIEDE...
...SEIJI-SAN, YAYOI-SAMA...
...HIKARU, KAORU, GRANDMA KOHARU AND HEIDI...
EVERYONE WAS HERE WITH ME.

BECAUSE YOU WERE THERE FOR ME.
ポロ
ポロ
KOUHEI...
...THANK YOU!

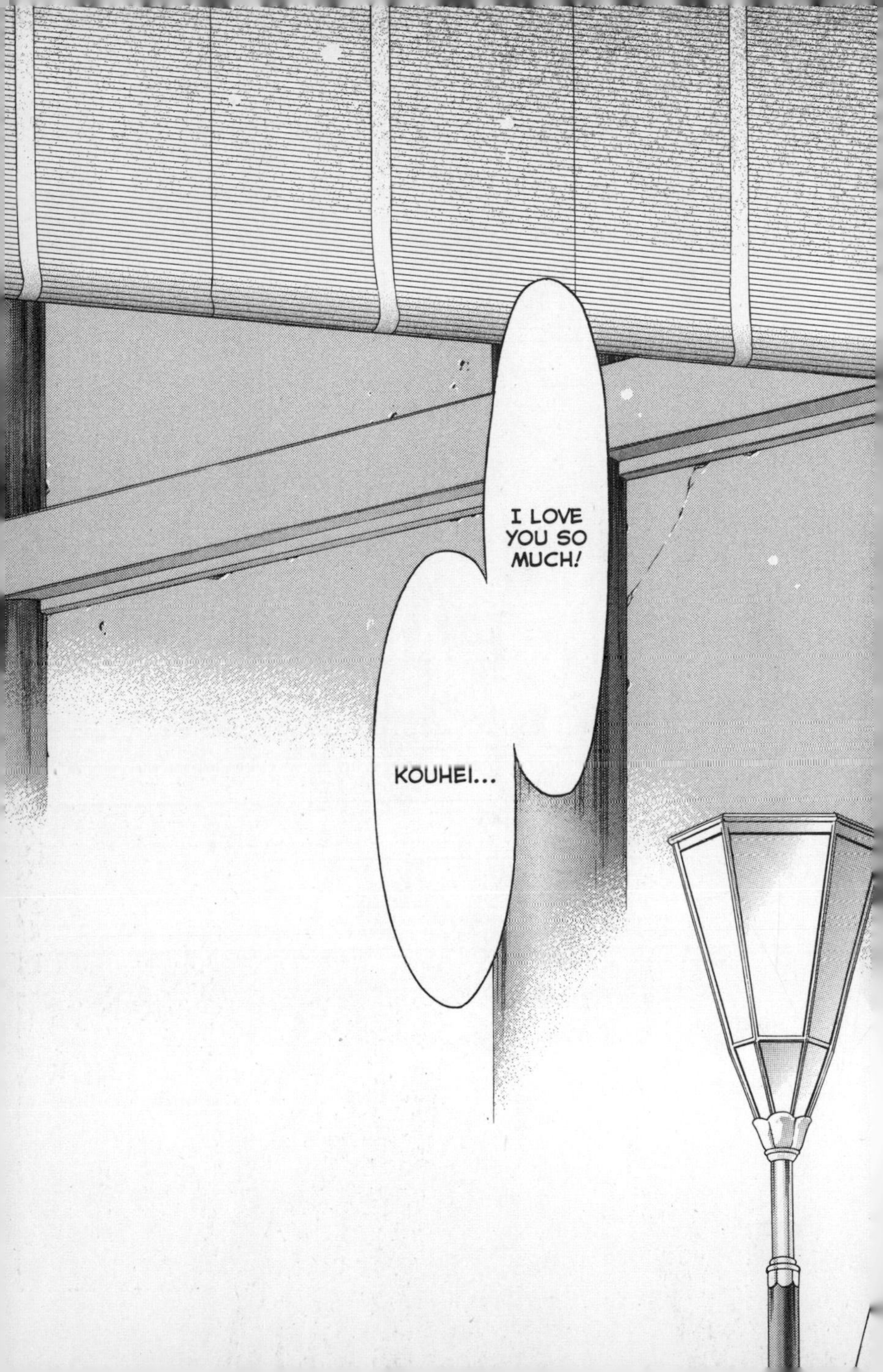
I LOVE YOU SO MUCH!
KOUHEI...

カタン…
DID YOU HAVE...
...ENOUGH TIME WITH HIM?
YAYOI-SAMA.
....
I SAID...
...GOODBYE TO KOUHEI.
THERE'S NOTHING MORE TO SAY.

LET'S GO...
...YAYOI-SAMA.
HAZUKI.
TAKE THIS WITH YOU.
?
WHAT'S THIS?
I JUST MADE IT, SO IT DOESN'T HAVE A NAME YET.

EACH PAPER HAS A LITTLE BIT OF SPIRITUAL ENERGY.
AND I CREATED IT TO RETURN TO ME WITH INFORMATION ON A LOCATION ONCE IT'S TAKEN OUT OF THE BOTTLE.
ALTHOUGH IT HAS NO POWER TO BUILD A KEKKAI BY ITSELF, IT WILL BE WELL-HIDDEN BECAUSE OF THAT.
IT WILL HELP US TRACK YOUR LOCATION, EVEN THOUGH IT MAY TAKE A LONG TIME.

YOU HAVE YOUR MASTER AND YOUR FELLOW DISCIPLES.
DO NOT FORGET THAT.
....
OKAY.
YAYOI-SAMA!
YAYOI-SAMA!
WHAT ABOUT ME?!
SEIJI, I WISH I COULD TAKE YOU AS MY WARRIOR...
...BUT I'M WORRIED ABOUT AN AFTER-EFFECT FROM THE INCIDENT.

IN CASE OF AN EMERGENCY, PLEASE CONCENTRATE ON...
...EVACUATING EVERYONE FROM HERE.
......
I UNDER-STAND.
I AM SORRY.
PLEASE TAKE CARE OF EVERY-ONE.

KAORU...

DON'T WORRY!
Ha ha ha ha!
HIKARU IS A TOUGH GIRL! SHE'LL MAKE IT BACK FINE!

GRAND-MA KOHARU...
I'M JUST GOING HOME AND HIKARU WILL COME BACK HERE. PLEASE DON'T WORRY.

WELL ...
I'M LEAVING NOW!

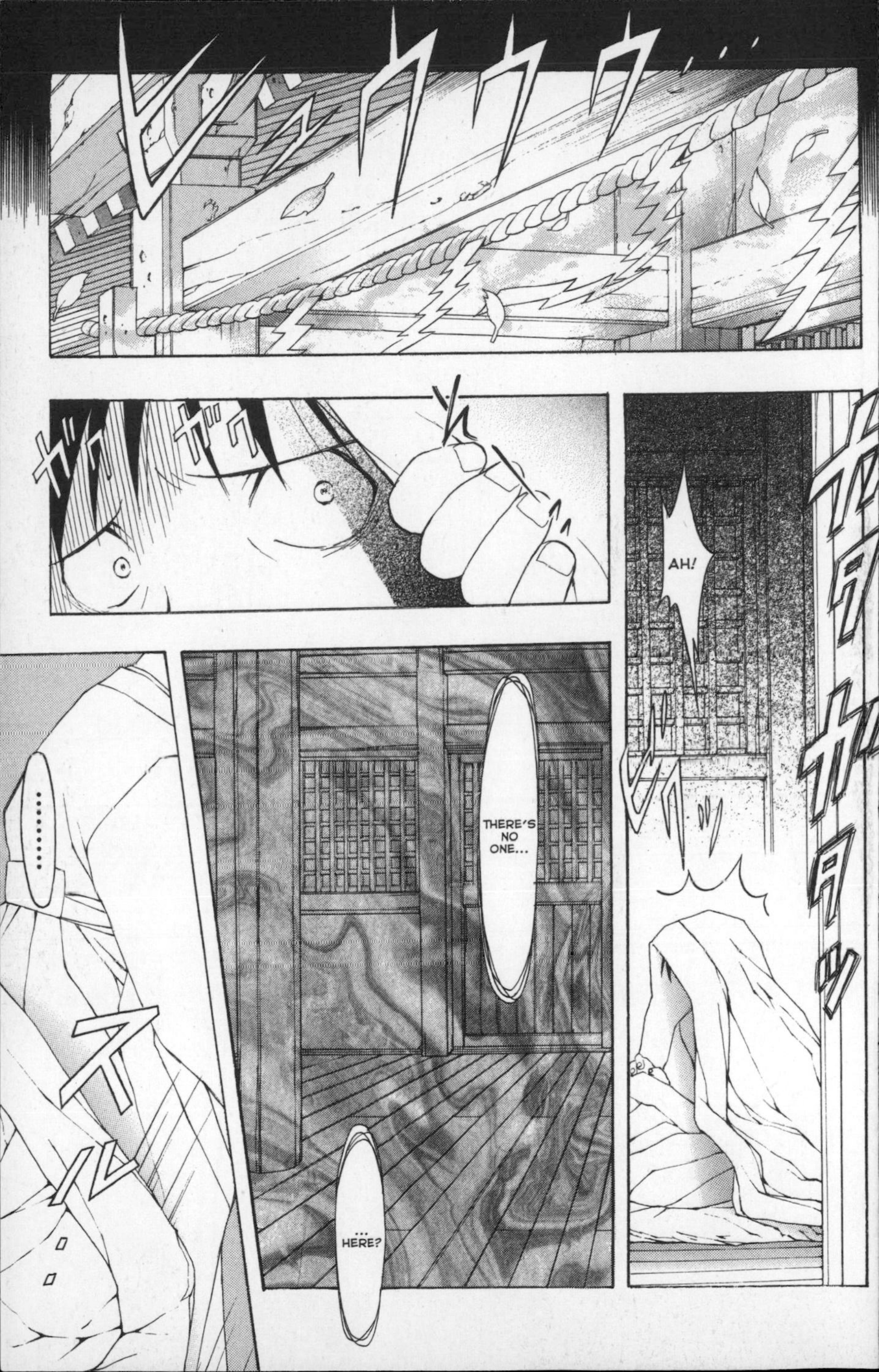
ヒュウウウ…
AH!
THERE'S NO ONE...
... HERE?
......

THIS PLACE IS ...
... SAFE.
THERE IS A KEKKAI BUILT BY YAYOI-SAMA.
A HOLY PLACE...
AND SHE'S NO LONGER ...
AH!
AH!
WAH!

AAAAAAH!
AAAAAAAAH!
WHO IS...
... "SHE" ?!
HUFF
HUFF
HUFF
HUFF
HUFF
HUFF

HUFF
HUFF
HUFF
WHO...
HUFF
...AM I?
HUFF
HUFF
ぬっ
ぬ
ゔゔゔ

WHO...
...ARE YOU?
HUFF
HUFF
WELL?
HUFF
TELL ME.
HUFF
......
HUFF
HUFF

WHO...
...ARE YOU?
WHO...
...ARE YOU?

Moon 月詠 Phase

Phase51
Kouhei, Awakening!!
己は一体何者なのか？
WHO ARE YOU REALLY?
―――
MY WHISPERING DOESN'T WORK ON A PERSON WHO IS READY TO FIGHT.
BUT SOMETIMES ONE WORD CAN WAKE UP THE POWER THAT IS HIDDEN INSIDE A PERSON'S HEART.

NOW ASK YOUR-SELF...
I'M SORRY.
...HOW YOU WANT TO BE.

I'M JUST TOO...
...SCARED OF YOU.

フラ
......
HUFF
HUFF
ヨロ
SLIP
WHOA!
カタカタッ
WAAH!
HUFF
HUFF
HUFF

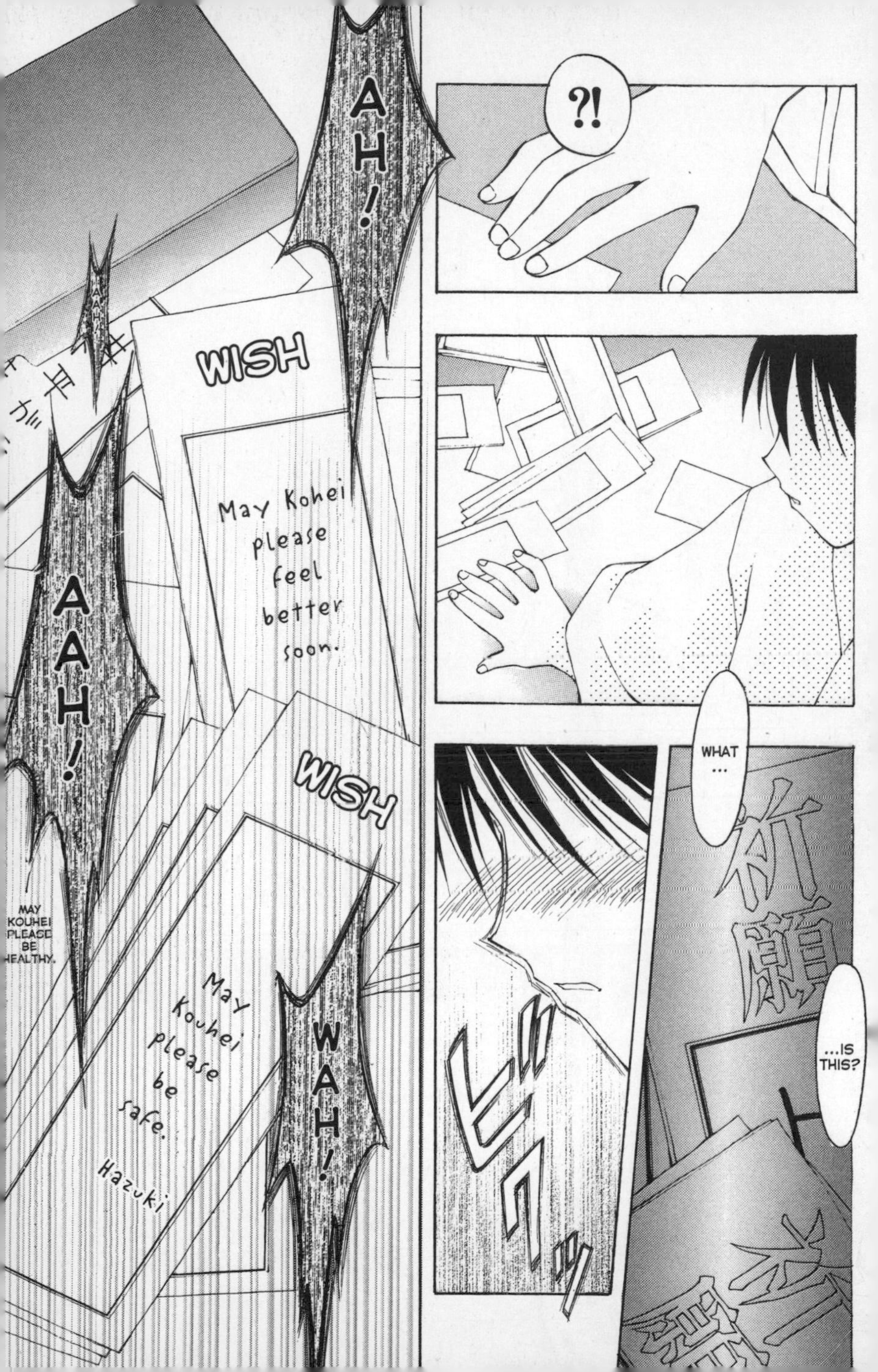
?!
WHAT ...
...IS THIS?
祈願
AH!
WISH
May Kohei please feel better soon.
AAH!
MAY KOUHEI PLEASE BE HEALTHY.
WISH
May Kouhei please be safe. Hazuki
WAH!

YOU WENT TO PRAY FOR KOUHEI AGAIN?
YOU ARE VERY SERIOUS ABOUT HIM, AREN'T YOU?
AH HA HA. IT'S GOOD EXERCISE!
CONSIDER IT TWO BIRDS WITH ONE STONE! ♡
WISH
healthy
I WANT TO AT LEAST PRAY FOR HIM...
...SINCE I CAN'T DO ANY-THING ELSE.

I HOPE...
...HE COMES BACK HERE SOON. ♡
AAAAAH!
WAAAAAH!

HEY!
ARE YOU OKAY?
WHY'RE YOU HOLDING...
...THOSE STUPID PAPERS?

......
DEATH! DEATH! DEATH! DEATH! DEATH!
Hya ha ha ha!
ヒヒヒ
Heh heh heh heh heh!
YOU'RE GOING TO DIE!!
DEATH! DEATH! DEATH!

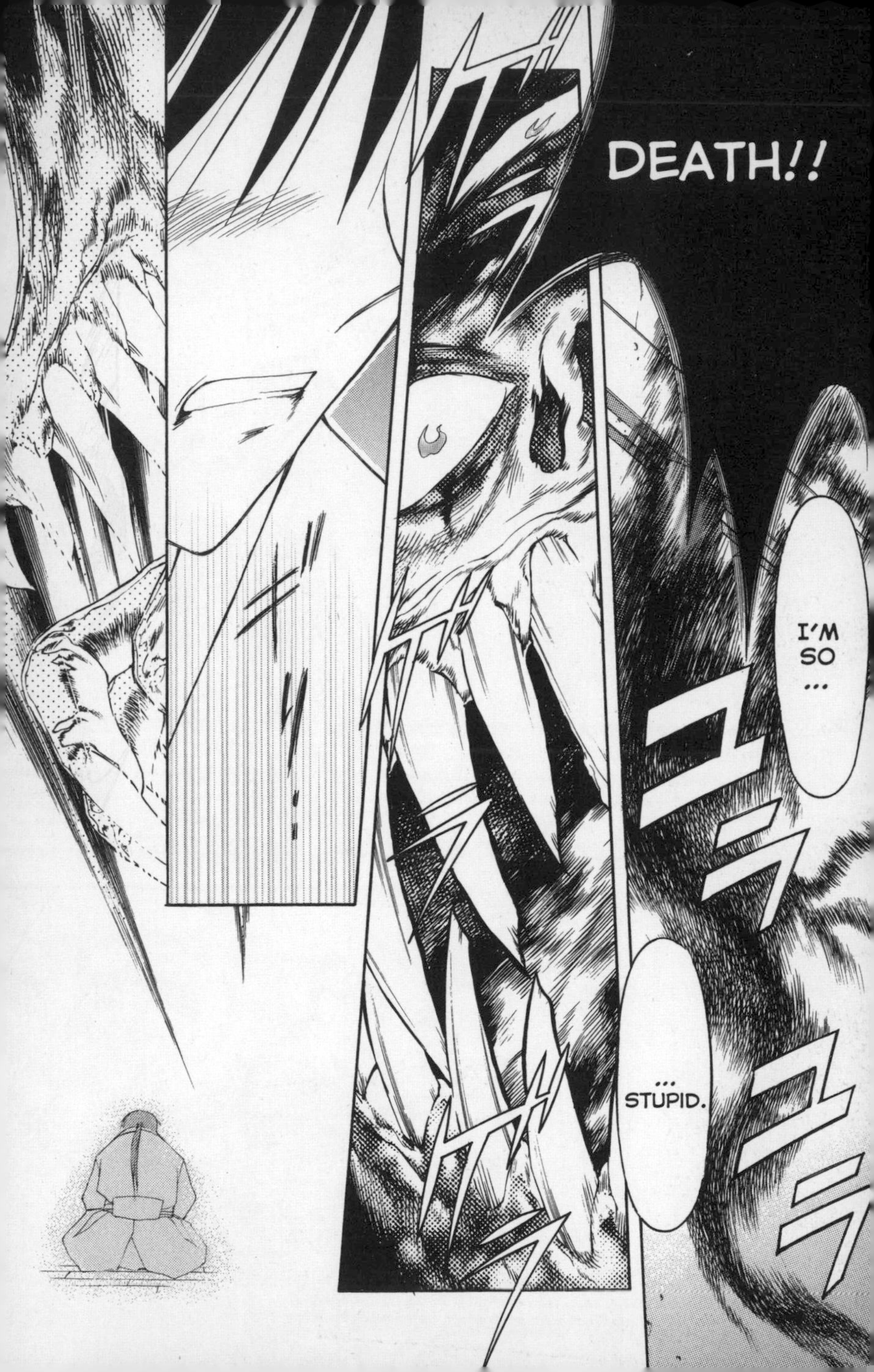
DEATH!!
I'M SO ...
... STUPID.

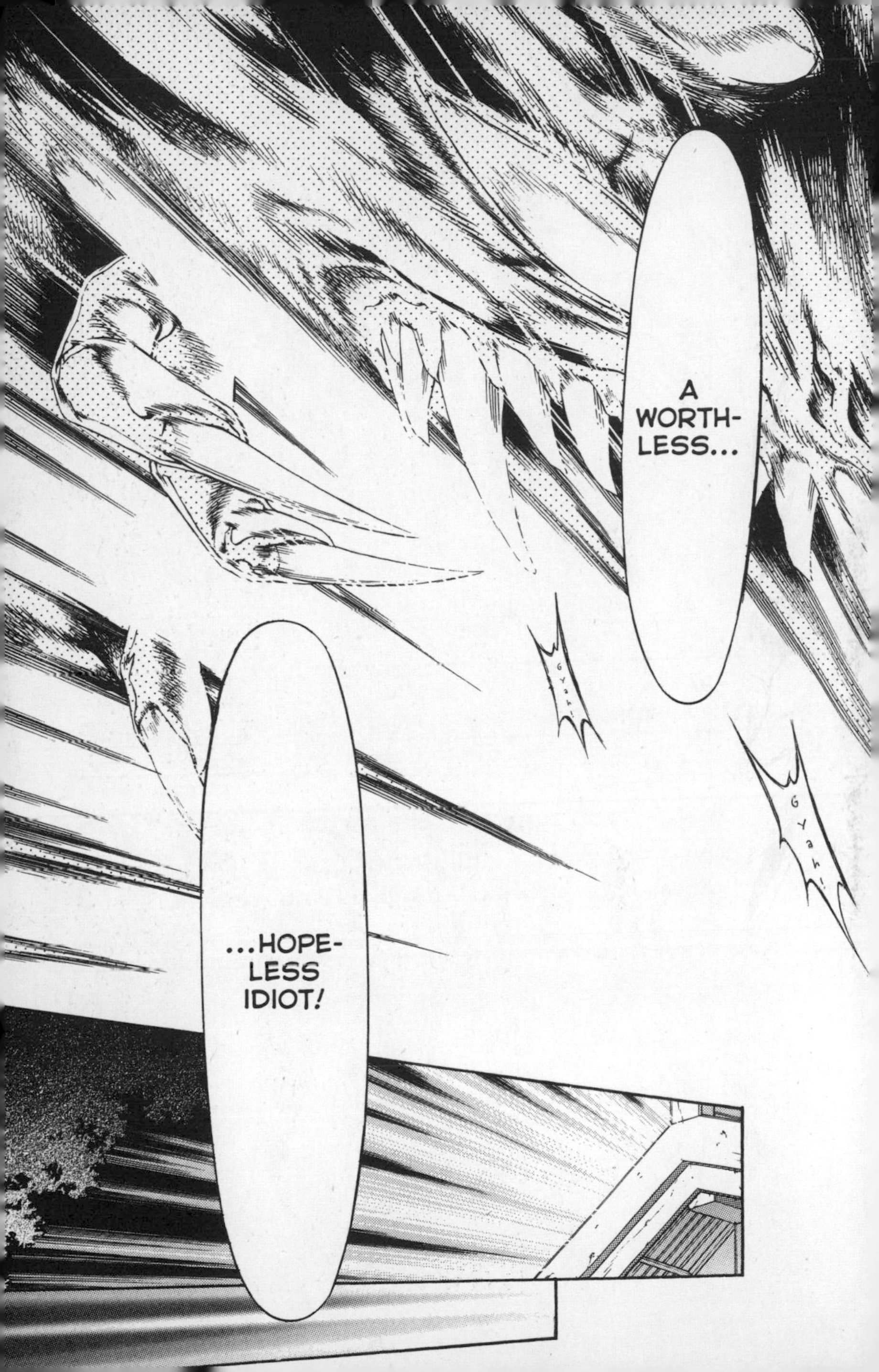

A WORTH-LESS...
GYah!
GYah!
...HOPE-LESS IDIOT!

Y-YAYOI-SAMA?!
AND HAZUKI?!
WHAT IN THE WORLD IS GOING ON?!
......
HEY!
NOW THEN...

AS WE PROMISED, WE WILL GIVE YOU BACK THE GIRL.
LADY LUNA. ARE YOU READY TO COME HOME WITH US?
YES.
GO!
WE DON'T NEED YOU ANYMORE!
EEEK!
HEY! WHAT'S GOING ON?
DON'T YOU GET IT?

?!
THEY NO LONGER NEED YOU BECAUSE I TOLD THEM I'M COMING HOME.

HEY, HAZUKI! WHAT HAPPENED TO YOU?!
BE QUIET! YAYOI-SAMA ALREADY APPROVED MY DECISION!

WHAT ABOUT KOUHEI-NIISAMA?!

......
KOU-HEI IS...

I ALREADY SAID...
HEY!
I NEVER SAID YOU COULD LEAVE!
?!!
...GOOD-BYE TO HIM.
......

KOU-HEI?!
YO!
I GOT HERE JUST IN TIME!
?!!

WHAT IS...
...THIS EVIL ATMO-SPHERE?
KINKLE ?!
NO. COULD IT BE... OYAKATA-SAMA?!

KOUHEI!
WHAT IS THIS ATMOSPHERE?
......
IT'S A WEIRD FEELING LIKE IT'S GOING TO JUMP ON ME EVEN THOUGH IT HASN'T TOUCHED ME YET.
IT'S MY DELUSION.
?!
I THOUGHT IT MIGHT APPEAR AGAIN ONCE I SAW YOU.
AND I WAS RIGHT!

IT'S TRYING TO SCARE ME.
IT'S SAYING I'LL DIE IF I STAY WITH YOU.
OR THAT I'LL GO MAD WITH FEAR.
GIVE ME A BREAK!
KOU-HEI?
I'D RATHER DIE...
...THAN BE WITHOUT YOU, HAZUKI!

WHAT?
WHAT IS THAT?!
AARGH!

NO WAY!
HE COULDN'T MAKE SUCH A LARGE EVIL SPIRIT DISAPPEAR, COULD HE?!
HAZUKI!
YES?!
SUCK MY BLOOD!
?!
WE'LL GO HOME TOGETHER AFTER DEFEATING THOSE GUYS!

OKAY! ♡
?!
I WON'T LET YOU TAKE HER AGAIN!
YOU WILL BECOME A PRISONER...
ha!
ha ha ha ha
...OF MY EVIL EYE POWER!
ha

TAKE THIS!
THE "BLUE EYES"?!
UGHH!
WHAT?!
?!

Huff
Huff
IS IT POSSIBLE ...?
MY EYE POWER DIDN'T WORK ON HIM?!

KOUHEI ...
OH?!
?!
SHOOT!
UGH!

UGHAAAAH!
PLEASE ...
...DON'T FORGET ABOUT ME.
Phase52
The Battle! Hazuki vs. Art

WHAT ?!
PRIN-CESS!
ALL I HAD TO DO IS...
...CUT THE KEK-KAI.

JEDA, QUIT PLAYING AROUND.
YES, PRIN-CESS.
WELL? ♡
SINCE LUNA SUCKED SOME BLOOD ...
...MIND IF I STEP IT UP, TOO?
ぺロ。。

WE HAVE NO CHOICE NOW. WE ARE ALSO THOSE OF THE MOON PHASE.
WE DIDN'T HAVE ENOUGH FUN TONIGHT.
LET'S EAT THE DINNER THAT WE COULDN'T EAT EARLIER.
Heh heh heh...
PLEASE BE CARE-FUL...
THEY ALREADY SUCKED BLOOD FROM SOME-WHERE.
THE DINNER THAT JEDA COULDN'T EAT EARLIER.

NOW...
...LET US SHOW THEM...
...HOW WE FIGHT TOGETH-ER!

KOU-
HEI?
YAYOI-
SAMA
?!

JEDA! TRY YOUR EVIL EYES ON LADY LUNA!
I'LL GO KILL THE REST!
YOU GOT IT!
YOU?! AGAIN?!
WHAT ?!
SUR-ROUD HIM!
KA-GOME!

AND CLOSE!
AAARGH!
KOU-HEI!
PROTECT HAZUKI!
OKAY!
HOW ...
...DID YOU ALL GET HERE?!

ARE YOU SUR-PRISED ?!
JUST LIKE BEFORE ...
... KOU-HEI MADE US...
HUH ?!
UGH!
... DISAP-PEAR!

AARGH!
BAST-
ARDS!
EEK!
HE
IS THE
ERASER...
?!
WHAT
...
...GREAT
TIMING!
UGH!
NO!
HIKA-
RU!

AH!
LUNA ...
?!
I WILL BE SCOLDED IF I KILL YOU.

SO I WILL MAKE YOU...
WAH ?!
... IMMOBILE!
HIKARU!

WHAT'S GOING ON?!
HA!!
THIS CAN'T BE HAPPEN-ING!
THIS GIRL ...
...CAN MOVE FASTER THAN ME?!
ARGH!

HEY!
HERE!
YO!
HA!
THERE!
TAKE THIS!
?!

DAMN IT!
KAMA-ITACHI!
AAAAH!!
IT DOESN'T WORK ON HER.

KAMAITACHI OR SPIRITS WON'T WORK ON HER SHADOW...
...SINCE HER SHADOW DOESN'T HAVE ANY THICKNESS.
I MUST DO SOME-THING.
?!
WHAT THE--?

SHOOT!
I CAN'T AVOID HER SHADOW!
HAZUKI!
I LOST MY BAL-ANCE!
OH, MY GOD!
I CAN'T MAKE IT!!
WAIT ...!

I CAN ERASE THE SHADOW!
AAARGH!
WHAT?!

KYAAAAAH!
?!

OH, NO!
PRIN-CESS!
DID KOU-HEI ...
DAMN ...
... YOUUU!
... ERASE HER SHA-DOW?!
NO WAY!
AAAARGH!

OUT OF MY WAY!
UGH!
PRINCESS!!
FORGIVE ME! I'VE FAILED AT PROTECTING YOU TWICE!
JEDA!
LET'S GO!
ROGER.
YOU... I WON'T FORGIVE YOU FOR HURTING OUR PRINCESS!

......
I'M SORRY ...
...I WAS LATE.
ペコッ
......

I WILL COME BACK TO EXACT MY REVENGE ON YOU!!

IDIOT!
STU-
PID!
DUMB!
PER-
VERT!
STUPID
FACE!
......

YOUR
FACE
...
...IS A
MESS.

UUH...
UUH...
THTOO-PID KOU-HEI!

Moon
月詠
Phase

IN THE NEXT

HOTELS, SWIMMING POOLS AND A LOT OF RELAXATION...OR AT LEAST THAT'S WHAT HAZUKI AND KOUHEI WERE EXPECTING. JUST AS THINGS SEEM LIKE THEY MIGHT SETTLE DOWN AT THEIR SECRET HIDEOUT, KOUHEI AND THE GANG MUST ONCE AGAIN RELOCATE TO AN ISLAND TO KEEP HAZUKI SAFE. ONLY ONE THING...VAMPIRES AND WATER DON'T EXACTLY MIX. TO MAKE MATTERS WORSE, THE SPECIAL CONNECTION THAT CONTINUES TO GROW BETWEEN HAZUKI AND KOUHEI IS BEING THREATENED, AND IT'S BY SOMEONE IN THEIR VERY MIDST...

CENTRAL ARKANSAS LIBRARY SYSTEM
SIDNEY S. McMATH BRANCH LIBRARY
LITTLE ROCK, ARKANSAS

TOKYOPOP®.com

WHERE MANGA LIVES!

JOIN the TOKYOPOP community:
www.TOKYOPOP.com

LIVE THE MANGA LIFESTYLE!

EXCLUSIVE PREVIEWS...
CREATE...
UPLOAD...
DOWNLOAD...
BLOG...
CHAT...
VOTE...
LIVE!!!!

WWW.TOKYOPOP.COM HAS:

- News
- Columns
- Special Features
- and more...

Battle of the Bands: © Steve Buccellato and TOKYOPOP Inc.

Available at the iTunes Music Store and everywhere music downloads are available. Keyword: TOKYOPOP

New releases every month! Check out these great albums AVAILABLE NOW!!!

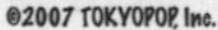

FOR MORE INFORMATION VISIT: WWW.TOKYOPOP.COM

FOR MORE INFORMATION VISIT: WWW.TOKYOPOP.COM

STOP!

This is the back of the book.
You wouldn't want to spoil a great ending!

This book is printed "manga-style," in the authentic Japanese right-to-left format. Since none of the artwork has been flipped or altered, readers get to experience the story just as the creator intended. You've been asking for it, so TOKYOPOP® delivered: authentic, hot-off-the-press, and far more fun!

DIRECTIONS

If this is your first time reading manga-style, here's a quick guide to help you understand how it works.

It's easy... just start in the top right panel and follow the numbers. Have fun, and look for more 100% authentic manga from TOKYOPOP®!